aloha
PatHall

CURIOUS KIMO

CURIOUS KIMO

story by
MALIA MANESS

illustrations by
PAT HALL

Pacific Greetings

Kamuela, Hawaii

Library of Congress Catalog Card Number: 93-86144

ISBN 0-9633493-0-9

First Printing, 1993
Second Printing, 1997

Available from:
Pacific Greetings • 65-1285 Puu Opelu Road • Kamuela, HI 96743
(808) 885-4439
e-mail: hlhall@ilhawaii.net

~~Pacific Greetings~~

Printed in Hong Kong

DEDICATED

to

our mother and grandmother

LEVERNE

our special

THANK YOU

to

RUTH TABRAH

for her help, encouragement, and editing

Four Hawaiian friends were walking through the forest one day.

"Where are we going?" asked Mynah Bird.

"What shall we do?" asked Mongoose.

"Lets play 'leap toad'!" said Toad.

"First," said Kimo Pua'a, "let's go find some nice juicy guavas to eat!"

As they went in search of guavas they came to a stone wall.

Toad turned around.

Mongoose turned around.

"Hey Kimo," said Mynah, "let's go back. Remember that your mother told you to never, never go past this stone wall."

"I know," said Kimo Pua'a, "but I'm just going to take a little peek to see if there are guavas on the other side."

Mynah squawked, "You shouldn't, Kimo. You really shouldn't."

But Kimo was climbing over the wall anyway, helped by a push from Mongoose.

"I'm coming too!" croaked Toad.

On the other side of the wall they
all stopped suddenly when they heard a
strange noise ...

VAARROOOOOMMM!

When they all went to see what the VAARROOOOOMMM noise had been, they stopped short at the edge of a big cliff.

"That looks dangerous to me, Kimo," Mynah scolded, "I told you we should not cross the wall!"

Mongoose said, "Let's go home, fast!"

"I'm scared," croaked Toad.

"I'm not scared. I smell a guava,"
said Kimo sniffing the air.

"I see a guava!" squealed Kimo, and
he leaned out on a branch that hung
over the edge of the cliff.

Suddenly his back feet slipped on the loose dirt and he almost fell to the road.

"You knocked down the guava!" squawked Mynah Bird.

"I'll get it for you!" yelled Mongoose.

"I'll go too!" Toad croaked.

Kimo hung on while Mongoose and
Toad ran down to get the guava for him.
They were just about to get it when ...
VAARROOOOOMMM!
Around the corner came a great
shiny blue monster with big glass eyes
and huge round feet. Mongoose and
Toad jumped out of the way just in time!

The blue monster ran right over the guava and squashed it flat. With one quick leap Kimo swung back to the grassy bank and he looked down at the smashed guava with its pink insides splattered all over the road.

The four friends stood looking down at the smashed guava.

"Look at that!" Mynah screeched. "That could have happened to you, Kimo."

"That could have happened to me!" said Mongoose.

"Me too!" croaked Toad.

Kimo was still shaking. "Mother was right," he said. "Roads are places to stay away from!"

Mynah rode Kimo's tail as they all
hurried back to the safe side of the wall.

"Look!" said Mynah, "Guavas!" He began pecking away at a ripe one himself.

"Delicious and safe!" said Kimo while chomping on one he picked up from the ground.

"BURP!" said Toad, as he happily swallowed a bug.

"Mothers are sure right about where not to go," sighed Kimo. "Weren't we lucky today?"